Beast Quest®

FALKOR
THE COILED TERROR

BY ADAM BLADE

ORCHARD

THE ICY PLAINS

THE NORTHERN MOUNTAINS

WESTERN OCEAN

THE FOREST OF FEAR

CONTENTS

STORY ONE

The wizards of the kingdoms gather in Avantia to welcome a new member. I will be there too, clapping like the other fools and wearing a phoney smile. But my heart is black, and my eyes are fixed on a greater prize.

A Beast stirs in the bowels of Avantia – a Beast who will do my bidding and unlock power unlike anything seen before.

The Circle of Wizards will be nothing when my plan is complete. Their pathetic spells and potions cannot save them.

And nor can their so-called hero, Tom. This will be one Quest too far for him and his pathetic friend, Elenna. Anyone who dares stands in my way will fall.

Cower, creatures of Avantia!

Your soon-to-be ruler

THE WIZARDS' CIRCLE

"Quickly, Storm!" Tom urged his horse forward, Elenna clinging on behind and Silver the wolf loping at their side. "We're very late – the ceremony may already have started!"

Storm had thrown a shoe, and it had taken a while to find a blacksmith to fix the problem. Then they had galloped all the way, desperate not to miss their friend Daltec's celebration. Today was the day he was finally accepted into the Circle of Wizards.

Storm crested the hill and Tom let out a relieved whistle.

"We made it," he said, staring in wonder and delight at the huge crowd gathered on the Central Plains.

The people of Avantia were dressed in their finest clothes and carrying many colourful banners. Near the centre of the crowd, on a raised platform, King Hugo and Queen Aroha sat on their thrones. A ring of soldiers circled an empty space at the very heart of the crowd.

"Can you see Daltec or Aduro?" asked Elenna, straining over Tom's shoulder. "And where are the other wizards from the circle?"

"Maybe they haven't arrived yet," Tom said, guiding Storm down the hillside with Silver trotting behind.

Daltec had been Aduro's pupil for a long time, and he had performed good service for the kingdom, but Tom knew that he would be the youngest wizard ever to be appointed to the noble circle.

Scanning the crowd with the far-sightedness given to him by his golden helmet, Tom pointed ahead. "I see Aduro and Daltec!"

The elderly former wizard and his apprentice were standing near the throne platform, dressed in heavy, formal robes embroidered with purple

and gold thread. The cheering crowds
parted as Tom and Elenna rode
through.

Tom leaped down, surprised to see
anxiety on Daltec's face.

"Where are the others?" Daltec

muttered, wringing his hands.

"Patience," Aduro said. "They will be here soon."

As Aduro finished speaking, a hush came down over the crowd and a chill wind swirled in from the east, snapping the banners. Storm snorted and stamped a hoof. Silver let out an anxious howl.

Something magical is happening, thought Tom.

A sheaf of dark clouds rolled swiftly across the sky. All eyes turned upwards as a funnel of cloud spread down towards the space kept clear by King Hugo's soldiers. The air shimmered.

There was a gasp from the crowd as a great stone building appeared, its circular walls towering over them, ringed with columns. Through tall arched windows, robed witches and wizards could be seen sitting at tables suspended at different levels.

The Chamber of Wizards!

Tom hadn't seen the chamber for a long time, not since evil Jezrin had sat at the Judge's Bench and sought to control the circle for his own wicked ends. He was relieved to see an elderly witch there now – surely a worthier leader for the Circle of Wizards.

Tom gazed around the chamber. He could see a few empty chairs. Aduro's, of course, and also Velmal's. He found his eyes drawn to the seat that used to belong to his enemy Malvel. He blinked in surprise. *Who is that sitting in Malvel's place?*

It was a white-haired young wizard, perhaps only sixteen years old.

"I've never seen him before," Tom murmured to Aduro, pointing at the young man, who was gazing around with eyes like chipped blue ice.

"His name is Berric," Aduro replied. "A talented sorcerer from Rion. Other members of the circle speak very highly of him."

Tom nodded, a sudden curious sensation coming into his mind. The red jewel in his belt had detected that a Beast was close by. He rose on tiptoes, gazing over the heads of the crowd, scanning the horizon.

There! A familiar figure on a lofty hill-top. Tagus the Horse-Man stood surveying his territory, his great arms folded over his brawny human chest.

He's the Guardian of the Plains, thought Tom. *It makes sense that he would be curious about what is happening here.* Tom touched the red jewel to speak to the Beast.

All is well, Tagus!

The Beast lifted his broadsword in acknowledgement.

Tom's attention was quickly drawn back to the chamber. The witches and wizards had risen from their seats and were descending to form two lines at the chamber's entrance.

Only the old witch at the Judge's Bench remained seated.

"Our greetings to Daltec," she intoned. "Your honourable heart and wise mind are most worthy additions to our circle."

Daltec walked between the double line of witches and wizards, his head humbly bowed. He proceeded to the chair that had once belonged to

Aduro. As he straightened his robes and sat down, the other members of the circle returned to their own seats.

Tom noticed Aduro wiping away a tear. *He's proud of his apprentice.*

"This is all a bit silly, don't you think?" Tom almost jumped at the voice that crawled into his ear. Turning, he saw Petra.

Tom frowned at the young witch. "What are you doing here?"

She winked, giving a sly grin. "Oh, I've just come for the feast."

Elenna gave her a cold look. "I'd say you're jealous because you haven't been allowed into the circle," she said.

Petra gave a hard laugh. "Me with that stuffy bunch of old fools?" she retorted. "I'd be bored to death!"

Tom eyed her, wondering if Elenna had touched a sore spot.

Daltec's voice rang out.

"I am humbled by the honour bestowed upon me by the circle," he said, raising his arms. "I will do my utmost to live up to your confidence in me!" So saying, he thrust out his hands and cast sparkling rainbow spells over the heads of the cheering audience.

Showers of rose petals rained down on King Hugo and Queen Aroha as they stood to applaud. Streams of firecrackers spurted from Daltec's fingers, crackling in the sky, chased by beams of bright light that twisted and whirled over the crowd.

Tom smiled as he watched Daltec's spells dancing above his head. But a cold and uneasy feeling came over him as the lights melted together to form the looming head and body of a vast, dark snake.

Fearful cries rose from the crowd as the snake plunged down, clouds of black smoke trailing from its mouth.

Tom glanced at Daltec – he was grimacing in anguish, his hands twisting in the air as though he was fighting to keep control of his own spell. His eyes widened in panic as the snake dived lower.

Something's wrong!

The snake of light and smoke whipped down over the crowd, wrapping around one of the columns supporting the entrance to the chamber. Its coils tightened and the

stone broke apart with a loud *crack*.

Tom stared in horror as part of the huge column began to topple towards the throne platform. King Hugo threw himself over Aroha's body.

They're about to be crushed!

AN ANCIENT EVIL

Tom called on the power of his golden
boots as he bounded towards the
platform. He took a mighty leap –
over the king and queen – landing
directly under the pillar, reaching up
as it fell towards him.

"Golden breastplate, don't fail me
now!" he gasped between gritted
teeth as he felt the weight bear down
on him. Every muscle in Tom's body

ached as he held the column up. The sweat poured down his face. He knew that even the power of the breastplate would only help him for a short time.

"Sire, get the queen away from here!" he panted.

Elenna bounded onto the platform,

pulling the king and queen to their feet and leading them to safety.

Tom dived sideways as the column thumped down. It missed him by a hair's breadth as it smashed through the platform. He sprang to his feet, jumping up on top of the column. Pandemonium had broken out in the crowds. People were screaming and running in all directions as the great sorcerous snake of light and smoke wove a destructive path through the Wizards' Chamber.

How can this be happening? Did Daltec really cause this chaos?

As their chamber was torn apart by the writhing monster, wizards and witches hurled bolts of fierce magic at it. But it seemed to absorb their spells, its coils looping around column after column. The snake flexed its body and more stone pillars cracked apart.

Tom drew his sword, ready to throw himself into battle. But without any warning, the terrible snake suddenly dissolved into wreaths of pale mist and vanished.

Tom saw the looks of shock and horror on the faces of the witches and wizards. Some turned to Daltec, their expressions angry and accusing. Broken stone rumbled as it settled. The chamber was utterly destroyed.

"Save my child!" came a terrible cry.

Tom turned towards the sound. A woman stood among the rubble, tears streaming down her face. Tom saw a small hand reaching out from between great chunks of stone.

There was a crumbling, crunching sound. The stones were still shifting. The trapped child could be crushed at any moment. Already people were gathering around the spot, but Tom realised they could easily do more harm than good.

Tom leaped down, bounding over fallen columns. As he ran, he used his red jewel to summon Tagus to his aid.

Daltec stood close by, his face grey with the horror of what had happened. Other wizards were trying to comfort the distraught mother. A little way off, the king and queen and Elenna were busy shepherding people away from the ruins.

Berric ran over, blue light flickering

at his fingertips. "Stand back," he said. "I will blast the stone away!"

"No!" Tom moved to block him. "That's too dangerous – the child could be hurt." He touched the groping fingers. "I'll save you," he said.

He heard the beat of hooves at his back, and an awestruck murmur from the crowd. Tagus had arrived.

Tom touched his jewel. *Tagus – can you hold that broken column steady while I pull these other pieces free?*

The great horse-man nodded, leaning down and circling the fallen column with his huge arms. Bracing all four hooves against the ground, he gripped it tight. Tom tore at the smaller pieces, creating a hole through which he was able to pull the

little girl to safety. There was joyful
relief in her tear-stained face.

"Thank you!" cried the mother,
taking the weeping child in her arms.
Tagus released the broken column
and it collapsed with a spurt of dust.

"I wasn't expecting all this entertainment when I invited myself…" Petra was right behind Tom again, smirking as usual. "Maybe Daltec needs to reread his spell book!"

Tom was about to snap at her for talking nonsense, when he saw that other wizards and witches were looking grimly at Daltec.

"What happened?" Berric demanded.

"I…I cannot explain," said the young wizard. "My spells were simple…for entertainment only…."

The witch in the judge's seat stood up. "Clearly, you are not ready to be brought into the circle, Daltec." She frowned at the young wizard, raising her hand high. "You are forbidden from using your powers. Go from here

while the rest of the circle considers
what punishment to exact." Her eyes
blazed. "It will be severe!"

"But I did nothing..." mumbled
Daltec, looking from Aduro to Tom.
"I'm innocent...I swear..."

"Daltec wouldn't have done this on purpose!"Tom cried.

"That's true," added Elenna, stepping up to his side. "He is honest and honourable!"

"Silence!" cried the new judge, raising her arms. "We will go now and debate this in private!"

A swirling wind came from nowhere, spiralling around the ruined chamber. There was a flash of white light and all the spinning rubble vanished. Tom blinked his dazzled eyes – every wizard and witch save Daltec and Aduro was also gone.

The crowds were making their way across the plains back to their homes, but King Hugo and Queen Aroha approached as Aduro placed his hand on Daltec's drooping shoulder.

"Aduro, you must speak to the circle on Daltec's behalf," the king said.

The old wizard shook his head sadly. "I have no influence, sire."

"Truly," mumbled Daltec, "I had nothing to do with that Beast."

Tom looked at Aduro. "Where do you think the snake came from?" he asked.

Aduro's face was grave. "I cannot say for certain," he said. "But I believe I recognised it. I fear that an ancient force has been awoken."

Tom gripped his sword. "Does it have a name?" he asked.

Aduro nodded. "Aye, it does. It is one of the first Beasts ever to be tamed, almost as old as Epos the Flame Bird herself – and it is named...Falkor."

THE WITCH'S PROMISE

A shiver of fear ran down Tom's spine as Aduro spoke the name of the ancient Beast. It stirred something in his memory. Elenna's face was ashen.

"I remember reading of him in the Chronicles of Avantia," she said.

Tom recalled it too, but only vaguely. "How can we help?" he asked.

Storm trotted up and nuzzled at

Tom's shoulder. Silver stood close to Elenna, his eyes watchful.

"Falkor was a Beast in the form of a great snake," Aduro explained. "He was ridden by a boy-sorcerer named Rufus. Rufus was a close friend to Tanner, first Master of the Beasts. For many years, they fought together on the side of Good. When Rufus died – an old, old man – Falkor also went to his rest, out of loyalty to his great friend."

"Falkor died?" asked Tom.

Aduro shook his head. "No. The Beast fell into a long, deep sleep."

Tom frowned. "So someone, or something, has now awoken him?"

"Indeed," said the wizard. "And only very powerful magic could awaken such an ancient Beast."

Tom clenched his fists – whatever the peril, he would face it down. "We have to learn who's behind this," he said.

"And prove Daltec's innocence," added Elenna, glancing at the unhappy wizard sitting close by with his head in his hands.

"Hunting down the source of such magic will not be easy," said Aduro. "But your best hope would be to start at Falkor's resting place."

"Do you know where that is?" Daltec asked.

"I do," said Aduro. "It lies deep in Avantia's Southern Caves."

That's in Ferno's territory, Tom thought, fondly remembering the fire dragon. *Perhaps I will be able to call on him for help.*

"Hey!" Elenna spun around, fitting an arrow to her bow. She aimed it where chunks of fallen pillars lay strewn about. "Show yourself!"

"What is it?" Tom asked.

"Someone is spying," said Elenna.

"Reveal yourself, or I will throw you into my deepest dungeon!" ordered King Hugo.

"No need to threaten me," said a shrill voice as Petra rose to her feet. "I wasn't eavesdropping – I was fixing my boots."

"Are you behind all this?" growled Elenna. "Did you raise Falkor from his sleep?"

"Good heavens, no!" exclaimed Petra as she strolled up. "Trust me, I'm as curious about this as you are."

Elenna's eyes narrowed. Tom knew his friend trusted the young witch even less than he did. She'd crossed their paths many times, and she always had her own agenda.

"Trust you?" he said. "After all the times you've shown you only care about yourself?"

"That's the old me," Petra said lightly. "I've turned over a new leaf." She looked at Tom and Elenna. "You don't believe me? Very well, I'll prove myself. I'll join you on your Quest for Falkor's bedchamber."

"I don't think so," said Tom.

"I'd rather we took a scorpion along with us," added Elenna.

Petra frowned, pointing to Storm. "So, you'll just trot along on your old nag for a few days, will you?" Storm snorted and stamped a hoof.

"Storm is no nag," said Tom. "He can run like the wind if need be."

"And I can cast spells that go even faster," said Petra, blue light flickering at her fingertips. "But if you prefer that Falkor runs riot through Avantia, have it your own way." She folded her arms. "Just don't say I didn't offer."

Tom glanced at Aduro, who was looking thoughtfully at the witch. He caught Tom's eye and nodded.

"Perhaps you have a point," Tom said. "We need to solve this mystery as quickly as possible."

A wide smile broke out on Petra's face. "You won't regret it," she said. "You have my promise."

"Play any tricks, and I'll be ready for you," warned Elenna.

"Tricks?" said the witch. "Me?"

Stepping forward, she raised her arms and clapped her hands.

Before Tom could react, a burst of black energy exploded from Petra's hands and the world went dark.

A DEADLY
AWAKENING

Air rushed in Tom's ears, as though
he was moving very fast through a
starless night. Then he felt as if he
was falling.

Cold water splashed over his legs,
and the darkness was gone.

He stared around. Elenna was at
his side, looking dazed. They were
knee-deep in swift-flowing water and

all around them hills and mountains reared against a blue sky.

"When you two have finished paddling, there's work to be done!" called a mocking voice. Petra stood dry-footed on the rock-strewn bank of the river.

Tom swallowed his annoyance as he and Elenna waded through the muddy water to the shore. If they were going to work together, he would have to ignore the witch's childish sense of humour.

"Where are Silver and Storm?" Elenna asked as they clambered out of the river.

"I'm good," said Petra, "but I don't have the power to move three people *and* two scraggy animals all this distance." She spread her arms. "Do you see where I've brought you?"

Tom nodded, looking around. He recognised the racing river and the barren foothills that humped up into the jagged brown mountain peaks. "This is the Winding River," he said.

"And that rocky hill over there is the entrance to the Southern Caves."

"Got it in one," said Petra, looking at Elenna. "And I didn't play any tricks on you."

"Except landing us in the river," muttered Elenna.

"Accident." Petra grinned, turning and marching towards the craggy brown hills.

The Winding River threaded its way between high shoulders of bare rock. Here and there on the flanks of the mountains, Tom saw dark patches, like scorch marks.

Elenna leaned close to Tom. "Why is she helping us?"

"Perhaps she really has changed?" Tom suggested.

"I doubt it," muttered Elenna.

A rough path led up to a cave mouth.

"What have we here?" said Petra, stooping.

Tom came up behind her. There were footprints – and they led into the cave.

"They're fresh," Tom said. "Someone has been here recently."

He put his hand to his red jewel, seeking out the fire dragon. *Ferno, are you there?* Something about this Quest made Tom uneasy. It was partly concern about having a tricky witch as a companion – and partly his memory of Aduro's worried look when he'd spoken of Falkor's power.

Ferno's deep, doom-laden voice echoed in Tom's mind.

You should not have come here, warned the fire dragon. *There is strange and dangerous magic in the caves. Turn back, friend of Beasts.*

Tom stared around in alarm. What kind of sorcery could frighten Ferno?

"What's wrong?" Elenna asked.

"Nothing," Tom replied. He didn't want to unnerve her with the truth.

Elenna gave him a doubtful look, but said no more.

"We'll need a light," muttered Petra, peering into the cave. She wriggled her fingers and a shining blue ball appeared in the air. She grinned at them. "No applause, please."

Tom heard Elenna give a heavy sigh as they followed the witch into the cave.

The ball of blue light floated along

the winding tunnel. The walls ran
with slimy moisture and green drops
oozed from the roof, making the
uneven ground slippery underfoot.

"Do you hear that?" Tom asked after
they had been walking in silence for
some time. The tunnel echoed with
the faint sound of a chanting voice.

"That's Old Avantian," Petra said.

"I bet neither of you understand Old Avantian."

Tom shook his head. "Do you?"

Petra huffed. "My parents had a book, but I never really read it." She paused. "There's something about 'waking' and something else about 'obeying'." She shrugged. "That's all I can make out."

They headed onwards, guided by the blue light. The voice was all around them, echoing off the walls, filling Tom's mind with deep foreboding.

At last, the tunnel opened out into a cavern, its high, soaring walls ringing with the chanting of the solemn voice.

Petra gestured and the ball of light floated into the middle of the cavern.

"What's that?" breathed Elenna.

Something huge was coiled on the floor of the cavern. At first it looked to Tom like a stream of lava that had looped and twined its way over the ground before cooling and becoming solid rock again.

But then he saw that the coils of rock were imprinted with scales. His gaze followed the curled shape, falling on a head with a wide mouth and great bulging, closed eyes.

"It must be Falkor," Tom said, his heart thundering in his chest. "I've heard of such things – ancient creatures turned to stone."

"Not for long," called a voice. "But you've arrived too late to stop the awakening."

Tom stared up. At the far end of the

cavern, beyond the huge fossilised snake, a cloaked and pale-haired figure stood on a high ledge.

"Berric!"

"You got here quickly with the help of the little witch," sneered Berric. "But not quickly enough. The spells are complete."

"You were behind the devastation at the chamber!" Tom shouted, drawing his sword.

"I was!" cried Berric. "The old fools needed teaching a lesson. They chose a decrepit witch as judge, when it should have been me!" He raised his hands, red light crackling at his fingertips. "I'm younger than them and far more powerful!" The fiery light snapped from his fingers,

scorching the air as it played over the coiled body of the immense snake.

Tom and Petra and Elenna were driven back by the heat of the writhing flames.

"You won't win!" Tom called angrily.

"Falkor was a Good Beast – as were all Beasts that befriended Tanner's companions!"

"Fool!" shouted Berric. "Falkor will follow whoever awakens him!" He stepped to the edge of the shelf. "Falkor!" he shouted. "Arise, my servant, and obey me!'

The red fires spread around the snake, flames licking up to the roof, forcing Tom and the others back into the tunnel.

The coiled snake glowed red, as though a furnace had been lit beneath its stone skin.

Tom heard Berric's harsh laughter, although he could no longer see the young wizard through the flames.

Then the fires died back and the

air cooled. Tom edged back into the cavern.

He stopped in his tracks, frozen in alarm – the tip of the snake's tail lifted into the air and then slapped down with a sound like a whipcrack. Then, slowly at first, the coils began to flex and move.

He's waking up!

Falkor's eyes flicked open and Tom found himself staring into huge black irises, rimmed with red flame. The head lifted, towering over Tom, the eyes bright and fierce.

And even as Tom raised his sword, Falkor uncoiled and came sliding silently forwards, his huge mouth stretched open to reveal fangs like bristling spears.

FIRE AND VENOM

Tom stood firm as the great snake
slithered forwards, his vicious tongue
flickering.

Falkor's scales shimmered, his long
tongue flickering menacingly. The
hissing that echoed from the massive
throat surrounded Tom, searing his
mind and filling him with doubt.

*Can I fight such an ancient
creature? He must have all the*

powers of the ages inside him!

Concentrating on the red jewel in his belt, he tried to enter Falkor's mind.

At first, there was only darkness and confusion, and then a burst of hatred and rage. He dug deeper into the Beast's mind, determined to communicate with it. But a shout from

the young wizard distracted him,
breaking into his thoughts.

"Falkor is mine! No one else will
control him!"

Tom glanced at Elenna. "You take
Berric," he said urgently. "Leave the
Beast to me!"

Elenna nodded, edging around

the curved cavern wall, fitting an arrow to her bow and firing it. The shaft glanced off the rock a fraction from Berric's head. She ducked as a blast of red light exploded from the wizard's fingers and cracked open the rockface where she had been standing.

"I'm coming too!" Petra ran forwards, her hands raised, blue flames dancing at her fingertips. But before she could fling a bolt of magic at the Beast, Falkor's long tail whipped at her, sending her crashing into the cave wall.

Tom saw the witch slide to the floor, the magical fire gone from her hands. There was no time to go to her aid. The Beast's huge head darted down at him, lightning-quick and deadly as a thunderbolt. Caught off balance, Tom flipped sideways as the gaping mouth hammered into the rock, the fangs spraying streams of thick yellow venom. The poison flowed down the wall, eating into the stone like acid.

Falkor drew his head back, hissing in frustration. His glazed eyes turned towards Elenna.

No!

"Falkor!" Tom shouted, clashing sword on shield to get the Beast's attention. "I have fought and defeated a hundred Beasts! Surrender now or face my anger!"

Falkor faltered, turning his head towards Tom, his eyes filled with centuries of malice and wrath.

Elenna slid along the wall, loosing another arrow at Berric. But the young wizard was ready now. With a wave of one arm, the arrow broke into fragments and turned into floating feathers.

Tom's eyes narrowed as Berric's laughter filled the cavern. The evil young wizard thought he had the best of them. Tom's jaw set – many enemies had thought the same, but he and Elenna had always managed to win through.

Falkor lunged, and Tom skipped aside, the edge of the Beast's jaw scraping his arm as the fangs bit once more into hard rock. Venom splashed high as Tom flung his shield up, its magic protecting the wood. He could

hear the poison sizzling all around
him, burning into the stone.

He bounded forwards, striking the
side of Falkor's head with the sharp
edge of his sword. The blade rang as
it glanced off the armoured scales,
the pain of the impact flaring through
Tom's arm and shoulder. The scales

were diamond-hard. Impenetrable.

"This is too easy!" cried Berric as the fiery hand grabbed another of Elenna's arrows and turned it into a shower of petals. "I cannot believe that you brought down the mighty Malvel!" Red flame danced on his hands, writhing and flaring as he drew back his arms and flung a gush of flame. Tom only just had time to raise his shield and deflect the attack.

And Falkor's head was lifting again, fangs dripping venom, eyes seething with savagery.

"Elenna! Get out of here!" Tom shouted, backing away as the huge snake moved in on him. "We can't defeat them like this!"

He saw Elenna sprinting for the

tunnel mouth. There was no sign of Petra or her ball of blue light. He guessed that the witch had recovered enough to run away.

Thinking only of herself – typical Petra!

Elenna hesitated for a moment at the entrance, clearly unwilling to leave Tom in danger. But he was at her side in an instant.

"We're not giving up," he panted as they ran into the tunnel. "While there's blood in my veins, I'll fight to free Falkor from Berric's influence!'

But as the two companions raced along the dark tunnel, Berric's triumphant laughter filled Tom's ears.

THE CLASH OF
BEASTS

Tom raced down the tunnel as Falkor
slithered after them, spitting venom.
He broke his stride, turning to jab his
sword at the Beast's glistening eyes.
Elenna fired an arrow, but it glanced
harmlessly off Falkor's scales.

"We can't make a stand here," Tom
gasped. "Run!"

They dashed along the tunnel.

Falkor slithered after them, head skimming the roof, long forked tongue flicking at their heels.

Tom had no plan – for now, his only instinct was to survive!

They came tumbling out onto the rocky mountainside. He saw Petra's globe of magical blue light hovering over a boulder close to the cave mouth.

"You coward!" Elenna shouted at the hiding witch. "Stand and fight!"

"*You* stand and fight," the witch retorted. "You're the so-called 'heroes'."

Tom turned to the cave mouth, shield up, sword ready. But Falkor hesitated in the tunnel, his eyes narrowing as he squinted at the floating ball of blue radiance. A grating croak came from the Beast's cavernous throat.

Uncertainty filled his eyes.

He doesn't like Petra's light – the witch is being useful, despite herself!

But could the Beast really be held off so easily?

"Petra, help us – we can drive him back using your magic!"Tom called.

"I'm not fighting that thing!" howled Petra. "I'll be killed!"

Tom heard Berric's voice call from behind the Beast: "Onward, Falkor! I am your master. Fear nothing!"

A thread of red fire burst from the tunnel, striking Petra's ball and destroying it.

Falkor surged forwards, all doubt gone from his blazing eyes.

The mouth gaped, fangs jutting forwards, dripping venom. Just in time, Tom jammed his shield between Falkor's jaws. His sword glanced harmlessly off the long fangs as they closed on the rim.

Tom struck again, desperately trying to wrench his shield free.

"Be careful!" he heard Elenna call.

"The tail!"

Too late, Tom realised what was happening – Falkor's tail had flicked forwards. It coiled around his chest, forcing his sword-arm down. Pain lanced through his ribcage as he struggled to get free.

Elenna sprang forward, jabbing an arrow between the scales of the Beast's tail. Falkor let out a stifled screech, but before Tom could escape, he saw a ribbon of red fire spurt from Berric's fingers.

"Elenna, no!"The flames struck Elenna, smashing her to the ground with an agonised cry.

The tail was squeezing so hard now that Tom couldn't catch his breath. Black spots flashed in his eyes as the excruciating pain built in his chest. A few more moments and he'd pass out.

He cleared his mind of the agony for a moment, concentrating all his willpower on the red jewel.

Ferno! He sent his thoughts out in desperation. *Help me!*

The coils pulled tighter until the pain in his ribs made him cry out. He could hear his shield creaking as Falkor's jaws clamped down. The Beast's ferocious eyes glared at him.

Tom's strength drained away. There was no air in his lungs. He could hardly keep hold of his shield. His sword arm was numb.

A dark shadow glided across the rocks – huge, winged, moving swiftly.

Ferno!

The fire dragon came soaring down, claws outstretched, roaring in anger.

Ferno's razor-sharp claws sank deep into Falkor's body. The snake-Beast writhed, howling in pain, his tail loosening around Tom's chest.

Tom lurched free, gasping for breath as he stumbled away. He dropped to his knees at Elenna's side, but her eyes were closed and she seemed to be unconscious – or worse.

He heard shrieking and roaring above him. Looking up, he saw Ferno and Falkor writhing and struggling in mid-air. Even as he watched, the lithe snake twisted around and its jaws clamped on the fire dragon's neck.

Ferno's wings faltered as he wrenched his head back, trying to

break free of the Falkor's grip. The two Beasts began to descend, still engaged in a death-battle. To Tom's horror, Ferno's voice sounded weak, agonised, in his head.

Pain! I feel the poison seeping into my blood!

The two great Beasts came crashing to earth, sending up a spray of splintered rock. Through the billowing dust clouds, Tom saw Falkor release the fallen dragon and slither off to where Berric stood, watching from the cave entrance with a vicious grin on his face.

Ferno? Tom's Beast ally wasn't moving at all.

"Now," Berric called, "I leave you to the mercy of the fire dragon!"

The wizard swept his hands in a circle, leaving a ring of red flame hanging in the air.

He's summoning a portal! He's going to escape with Falkor.

Tom turned at a clatter of claws. Ferno had risen to his feet, his wings spread wide, his head stretched forward on his long neck.

"Ferno?" cried Tom.

The Beast's eyes burned with a hideous red fury, and Tom understood what Berric had meant. Falkor's venom had somehow infected the Good Beast.

Ferno reared up, smoke rolling from the sides of his mouth.

Tom stared in horror as the jaws opened wide. He saw flames building up in the fire dragon's throat.

"Ferno, don't!" he cried.

He flung himself aside as flames burst from the Beast's mouth. Shrouded in billowing smoke, Tom called on the power of the dragon scale, embedded in his shield, to drive the fires back.

From the corner of his eye, he saw Petra cowering behind a boulder.

"You have to stop Berric!" Tom shouted to her. The wizard's portal had formed – a dark hole hanging in the air. Berric and Falkor were at its threshold.

Petra flung out her arm. A bolt of blue lightning sizzled through the air, hitting Berric between the shoulder blades and sending him crashing face down on the ground, unconscious.

At the same moment, the flames

gushing from Ferno's mouth died away and the light in his eyes faded.

The fire dragon had only attacked because Berric had been controlling him. Now that the wizard had been

struck down, Ferno was free.

Hissing and spitting, Falkor reared up, his angry eyes fixed on Tom. A hideous voice stabbed into his mind.

You will pay for this! All of Avantia will pay!

Falkor's tongue flicked out, looping around Berric's waist and lifting the wizard up. Still glaring, the snake-Beast slithered towards the portal.

"Stop him!" Tom shouted. "He's going to get away!"

But it was too late. Before Petra could conjure another spell, the serpent glided through the portal. Tom was only halfway to the black hole when it vanished in a curl of dark smoke.

Falkor was gone.

THE END OF ALL
GOOD MAGIC

Tom turned to Elenna, fearful that
she had been badly hurt. But to
his relief, he saw her lift her head,
grimacing as she struggled to sit up.

He helped her to her feet, looking
anxiously at her as she winced and
clutched her side.

"I think I may have cracked a rib or
two," she gasped.

"Stand still." Tom took Skor's green jewel from his belt and rested it against Elenna's side. As the power of the jewel knitted Elenna's broken bones, Tom watched Ferno, ready to fight if the fire dragon attacked.

Ferno shook his head slowly from side to side, his eyes blinking in confusion. The Beast's remorseful voice filled Tom's head.

I do not know what evil power possessed me!

Falkor's venom made you Berric's slave, Tom assured the Good Beast.

"Is that dragon going to behave itself now?" asked Petra, sidling up to Tom.

"Ferno is fine," Tom said. "Thank you for saving me."

Petra shrugged. "Now we're even,"
she said. "You were foolish to let
Berric get away. If his plan works,
we'll probably all die."

Elenna looked at Petra. "His 'plan'?
And how do you know about that?"

"I understood part of the spell he

used to open the portal," Petra said. "The portal was a doorway to the ancient fortress of Rufus."

"Tanner's friend?" exclaimed Tom. "But why would Berric go there?"

"To get the Scythe of Power," explained Petra. "Don't you know anything?"

Tom swallowed his irritation once again. "Tell us," he said.

"The scythe was Rufus's great weapon," Petra explained. "It has the power to steal the magic from all other witches and wizards."

Tom stared at her in alarm. "That must never happen," he said. "If a sorcerer like Berric controlled all the magic in all the known realms, he would be invincible!"

"The scythe is kept in the highest chamber of the fortress," Petra continued, raising an eyebrow. "You ought to know it's surrounded by a maze that no living person can find their way through." She gave Tom a gleeful smile. "They say a hundred heroes have died trying."

"So how does Berric intend to get to the scythe?" asked Elenna.

"Falkor knows the way, because of his ancient ties to Rufus," said Petra. "The Beast will lead Berric to the high chamber." She nodded. "They're probably halfway to the scythe as we speak."

Tom felt a surge of anger. A Beast should never be used for such a wicked purpose. "How do we stop him? Can you open a portal to the fortress?"

"Possibly," Petra said. "If I can remember the spell correctly."

"Try!" demanded Tom. "Prove that you really have turned over a new leaf."

Petra sighed. "I'll do my best," she said. "Of course, you realise that if I get some words wrong, you'll probably end up somewhere else…" She grinned. "Somewhere quite nasty – like in the middle of an erupting volcano, or at the bottom of the sea!"

Tom shared an uneasy glance with Elenna. Was this one of Petra's bad jokes, or might they really find themselves in such deadly peril? "I'll take that risk," he said. *What other choice do we have?*

"Stand back." Petra said, her voice suddenly loud and commanding. Tom and Elenna moved away from her as she began to make passes in the air with her hands, her fingers leaving trails of blue light.

"Vaults of night and caves of fright, spears of light and spells of might," Petra chanted. "No, wait!" She knitted her brows. "Or was it 'vaults of fright and caves of night'...?" She shook her head. "Hmmm. Tricky."

"Petra!" shouted Tom. "The fate of the kingdom depends on this!"

"I know," Petra said crossly. "Give me a moment. Yes...it was definitely 'vaults of night'." She began to chant again, her voice growing more confident as she spoke the age-old spell.

And as she chanted, the threads of light coming from her fingertips darkened and swirled.

"You did it!" cried Elenna as a black portal formed in the air.

Petra wiped her sleeve across her forehead. "Phew! That was hard work." She gestured towards the black hole. "Off you go, then. Good luck."

Elenna looked at Tom. "How can we be sure this portal leads to the fortress of Rufus?" she asked.

"Seriously?" asked Petra, hands on her hips. "Will you ever start trusting me?"

"I doubt it," muttered Elenna.

"I know she can be treacherous,"

Tom said. "But this time, she's our only hope. If Berric gets the Scythe of Power, every kingdom will be in danger."

"Exactly," said Petra, stepping aside from the portal. "I don't want to live in a world ruled by a madman like Berric. You can trust me this once – Rufus's fortress lies at the other side of this portal."

Tom stepped up to the black sphere. Elenna stood at his side, still giving Petra uneasy looks.

"You're coming with us, Petra," Tom said, drawing his sword.

The witch laughed. "I'm happier staying here."

Tom and Elenna glanced at one another. She winked.

"What are you planning?" asked
Petra uneasily.

Tom nodded, and they lunged at the
witch, grabbing an arm each.

"Hey!" yelled Petra, struggling as
they pulled her towards the portal.
"Let me go! This is kidnapping! I'll

report you to...yoww!"

Clinging on firmly to the wriggling witch, Tom and Elenna stepped into the portal. A rushing darkness surrounded them.

The next stage of their Quest was about to begin.

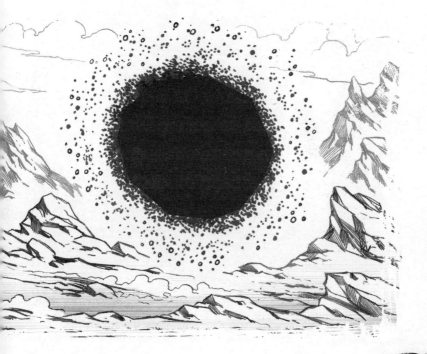

STORY TWO

And so it comes to pass, just as I planned. The scaled Beast is a slave to my wishes. How I laughed to see the Wizards' Chamber crash to the ground. All those terrified faces!

But if they think that is the end of their ordeal, they could not be more wrong. Falkor has brought me to an ancient, magical place, and soon I will wield the Scythe of Power. After that, no spells, no warrior, no jealous foe can stop me. I will have all the magic of all the kingdoms at my fingertips.

As for that cretinous boy Tom and his companions, they will have the honour of being my first victims. I will kill them slowly.

Do stay and watch their misery – if you dare...

Berric

THE ICE MAZE

Tom stared around himself, his breath clouding in the frosty air. The witch's portal had brought them to a snow-clad mountain landscape.

He and Elenna still held Petra's arms, but the witch had stopped struggling. They were facing a long smooth wall of ice that stretched away in either direction. There was no sign of Berric or Falkor.

"Thanks for bringing me here!" The witch pulled free, wrapping her cloak around herself. "I just love the cold!"

The wall was maybe twice Tom's height. Not a difficult jump, if he used the power of his golden boots.

"This is the outer wall of the maze," Petra said. "But don't get any ideas of climbing it – that's against the rules."

Tom wondered what she meant
by that.

Far beyond the top of the wall, the
upper ramparts and battlements
of a huge white castle were visible,
its soaring walls rising to pointed
pinnacles and turrets.

It's older than anything I've ever seen!

A long stone stairway wound up the

outside of the fortress, snaking all the way up to the highest tower.

"Remember, I told you Falkor knows the way through the maze," said Petra. "They're probably at the other side already." She eyed Tom. "We should go back. We'll never stop them now."

"Be quiet!" snapped Tom, searching the ice wall. A little way to their left, he saw an arched door of pure ice. He ran towards it.

No handle! How does it open?

He pushed and the door swung open with a rush of chill air.

"Let's go," he said, turning to Petra. "You, too. We might need your magic."

Reluctantly, Petra followed the two companions through the door. It slammed shut at their backs. They were in a long curved corridor with rearing ice walls. Streams of fine, chilling mist wafted off the walls, gathering in numbing pool of fog that swirled around their feet.

"Which way should we go?" Elenna asked, her breath a gusty white cloud.

Tom knew they had no time to waste. They would have to rely on instinct and guesswork. He picked a direction and began to walk, Elenna and Petra following close behind.

He came to another door. It swung open at a touch, leading to another corridor of ice. He turned right and ran, a terrible urgency burning in his heart. *Berric and Falkor may already have entered the fortress.* Every moment was precious.

He shouldered through another door into another set of snaking corridors, zigzagging and looping back on themselves. Tom had no idea whether they were moving towards the fortress or away from it.

He came to a blank wall of impenetrable ice. This corridor had led him nowhere. He turned, pushing past Elenna and Petra, running faster, diving through another doorway.

The corridor beyond ended in a blind sheet of ice. In frustration, he drew his sword and struck the wall.

"I wouldn't do that if I were you," said Petra, coming up behind him. "The maze gets cranky if people break the rules."

"You make it sound as if the maze

is alive," said Elenna.

"It's full of old sorcery," said the witch. "I can feel it."

"I have to know where we are," Tom muttered.

He crouched low then jumped. The magic of his golden boots sent him soaring up onto the top of the wall.

He could see the maze spread out below him, coiling around the foot of the fortress like a serpent. He knew the yellow jewel in his belt would help him memorise the route. A moment later, the wall lurched under him and he lost his balance, falling down into the narrow corridor.

"Did you see anything helpful?" Elenna asked as he got to his feet.

"I did," Tom said. "I know the way."

"You'll regret doing that," insisted Petra. "Listen. The maze will punish us. See how it threw you just now?"

"I'll do whatever it takes to get to Berric and Falkor," Tom said firmly. "If the Golden Armour gives me an advantage, I'll use it."

"It's your silly Quest," Petra said

with a shrug. "But don't say you weren't warned."

Tom ignored her. The layout of the maze was clear and precise in his mind. He pushed through a door, turning left along the corridor.

We'll be out of here soon!

A low rumbling echoed along the corridor.

"What's that?" asked Elenna.

"Punishment," groaned Petra.

Tom and Elenna looked anxiously at one another.

The ground shook under their feet, the high ice walls trembling around them. Tom drew his sword, turning to face the oncoming danger.

What's making that noise?

As though in answer to his

thoughts, a massive boulder of ice came barrelling around the curve of the corridor. Its sides scraped the walls as it careered towards them.

"I told you so!" shrieked Petra, bolting as the boulder gathered speed.

It's huge! We'll be crushed!

"Go!" cried Tom.

As he and Elenna sped after Petra, Tom scoured the walls for doors – but there were none. They were trapped between walls of ice and at every moment the boulder gained on them.

Petra turned for a moment, flinging her arm back and shouting some kind of spell. Tom and Elenna had to duck as a shard of blue light seared over their heads. In her panic, the witch had almost hit them. The fizzing

light struck the boulder with a crash, creating a blizzard of ice fragments.

Petra came to a skidding halt, staring at the smashed remnants of the ball. "I didn't think that would work!" she gasped. A moment later, she frowned. "Can you hear that?"

More rumbling. From the same

direction. Getting closer.

A second ice boulder came careering down the corridor.

Petra took a deep breath and flung lightning at it. The boulder exploded.

But the rumbling noise continued. Now a third boulder was pounding relentlessly along the corridor.

Breathing hard, Petra flung another bolt. Tom saw that it was weaker than the others. The boulder cracked but kept coming. Petra threw another spell – it slowed the boulder down, but didn't stop it.

The witch's powers were fading.

"Run!" shouted Tom.

Petra dropped to her knees. The spells had exhausted her. Tom grabbed her, heaving her back to her feet and stumbling after Elenna, who had raced on ahead. Her voice sounded from around the next corner.

"I've found a way out!"

Tom towed Petra along, using the golden leg armour to move as fast as he could. They took the corner, seeing Elenna holding a door open. Tom took a firm hold of Petra's arm to pull her through the doorway as the great ice boulder went crashing past them. Elenna followed them in, letting the door swing closed.

As the rumbling sound faded, Tom got to his feet, gasping for breath.

"Oh, no!" Elenna despaired.

Tom looked around. They were outside the maze – back in the very place where they had started!

2

THE TRAP SHUTS

Tom stared up at the fortress. Two shapes were moving on the long winding stairway – one small, the other huge. Just as Petra had warned, Falkor had found his way through the maze, and the wizard and the Beast were climbing to the chamber of the Scythe of Power.

Tom growled in frustration. "We've wasted all that time!"

"I told you not to bother," said Petra. "Much as I admire and adore you," she continued with a barely concealed snigger, "I'm finished helping you out on this ridiculous Quest."

Elenna glared at her. "If Berric succeeds, he will take all your magic away," she said. "Doesn't that bother you?"

Petra shrugged. "I'd rather be an ordinary girl than a magic girl squashed by a giant snake."

"Go, then!" Elenna cried. "Tom and I will finish this Quest together – the way we always do."

Petra grinned. "Good luck with that," she said.

Tom opened the door into the maze

and Elenna followed him through.

"At least this time I know the way," he said. "But we have to move quickly."

They ran, threading their way along switchback corridors, through doorways and past blind off-shoots that Tom knew led nowhere.

"This way now." Tom dashed down a long curving corridor. If his mental map was accurate, they were more than halfway through the maze.

Yes! He remembered this! *Run to the left. Through the second door. Turn right. Past five doors. Take the left fork.*

"Around this curve," he told Elenna, "the corridor divides. We go right."

He heard a strange grinding sound

up ahead. Puzzled, he raced around the bend and crashed headlong into an ice wall. He reeled back, his head throbbing.

That shouldn't be there!

The fork he had been expecting was right in front of him – but the turn they needed was blocked with a barrier of ice.

"Are you sure you remembered correctly?" asked Elenna.

Tom paused, doubting himself for a moment. "No." He shrugged off his uncertainty. "But Narga's yellow jewel has never led me wrong in the past." He glared at the impenetrable wall. "The maze is changing itself to stop us!" He shut his eyes, filling his mind with the map. Was there another way to the centre?

Yes! "Follow me."

He pounded along the corridor, determined to slip through before the maze could stop them.

Griiiinnnddd.

He came to a stumbling halt. Ahead of them, the ice walls had pushed together, leaving only a narrow slit.

"The maze isn't going to let us past," gasped Elenna as they backed up.

Tom fought against anger and frustration. The maze was designed to baffle intruders. He had to keep a level head. The map in his mind was useless if the maze kept rearranging itself, but perhaps there was a way to trick the maze!

"I'm being punished because I broke the rules," he explained to Elenna. "If we split up, you might get through." He thrust out his hand, looking his companion in the eyes. "Good luck."

Elenna took his hand. "Good luck,

Tom," she replied. "If I succeed, I'll call out to let you know how."

She quickly turned and ran down the long curve of the corridor. He watched her for a few moments, the battles they had fought side by side passing swiftly through his mind.

Will I ever see my best friend again?

Losing Elenna would be like having his heart torn out. But she was smart and brave. *She can do this*, Tom told himself.

He turned, opening a door and running through, then choosing a corridor that led in the opposite direction from Elenna.

"I think I'm heading the right way," he heard her shout.

"If you get out first, be wary of

Berric," Tom called back. He opened a door, hearing the grind of shifting walls closing behind and in front. The maze was working hard to stop him, but for every route its shifting walls blocked, another opened up.

Tom could hear Elenna's voice every now and then, but she sounded a long way off and he could hardly make out what she was saying.

Almost there! I'm sure of it!

With a grating shriek, an ice wall slashed across in front of him. He spun on his heel, his heart pounding.

A second wall blocked his way back. He was in a prison of ice, unable to go forward and unable to retreat.

"You don't beat me that easily!" he muttered, flexing his legs, drawing on the power of the golden boots to jump free.

But even as he launched himself into the air, the ice walls stretched up to twice their original height. Tom scrabbled at the walls, but his fingers couldn't grip the smooth surface and he fell back to the ground.

"Tom!" Elenna's voice was faint. "I think I'm almost there!"

He was about to call back when the ground shook under him and a low scraping noise filled his ears. A terrible dread froze Tom's heart. The walls were closing in on him.

He crouched and jumped again, summoning every ounce of magic from the golden boots. But it wasn't enough. He smashed against the towering wall and fell back with a shout of despair.

The ice walls were moving in steadily.

Using his own strength and the power of the golden breastplate, he braced his arms against the grinding walls. Pain flared through his shoulders, his muscles screaming. He turned, shoving his back to the wall, bringing his feet up to try and fend off the other one.

It was useless.

He could feel his bones grinding together. The excruciating pain filled him with despair. He had been too confident. He had underestimated the power of the ancient magic that haunted this place – and now he was

paying the ultimate price. Petra was
right.

It's over – I've failed!

FLAMES OF THE SCYTHE

Tom's breath came in ragged gasps as his heart hammered against his creaking ribs. The walls closed like the jaws of a vice. This was no Beast to be fought and defeated – no sword or shield could stop the deadly advance of the ice.

Suddenly the pressure eased. Tom gulped in air, hope growing in him as he pushed against the walls with all his strength.

Had the magic failed?

The walls softened, yielding at his touch. Chilling drops fell around him as water streamed down the walls. Cracks spread, slivers of ice falling away. Freezing water rained on to his head and shoulders. The walls were melting, hard ice turning to drenching torrents. A moment later, the walls burst apart in a flood of bone-numbing water, thundering down, swirling around him and ripping him off his feet.

At last the flood ebbed away and Tom was able to get up.

The entire ice maze was gone.

"I didn't know that would happen!"

Tom spun around at the sound of Elenna's voice. She was standing under the outer walls of the great fortress, a long rusty metal lever in her hands. "I just pulled it in the hope it would do something useful."

Tom's chest swelled with relief – Elenna had found her way through the maze, and she had saved him from certain death!

"That was impressive!" There were splashing sounds as Petra came racing across the slushy ground. "The lever must be a fail-safe device."

Tom stared up at the towering fortress, his keen eyes following the line of the winding stair. He saw that the stairway emerged from the top of a gatehouse, looping and looping around the fortress walls like a snake coiling to engulf its victim.

He strained his eyes to look higher and higher, but there was no sign of Berric or the Beast on the stairs.

"They're inside!" Tom cried, running for the gatehouse with Elenna and Petra close behind. "We have to stop them!" The high entrance loomed over him, ancient and ominous – Tom could only imagine how many heroes had died seeking this gateway into the unknown.

He halted a few paces inside the gatehouse, staring up in astonishment. The hollow interior of the fortress consisted of galleries and walkways and terraces and balconies, soaring away to dizzy heights,

supported on clusters of tall pillars.

At the very pinnacle of the fortress, Tom saw a stone platform under a vaulted roof. The stairway swept in from an opening high in the wall, ending at the platform. There was no other way up there.

On the platform stood a statue of a bearded old man whose stone hands gripped the Scythe of Power, resting it on his shoulder. The eyes in the stern face were fierce, as though daring anyone to wrest the scythe from his grip.

"That's Rufus," Petra said, her voice echoing. She pointed at a figure on the top of the stair. "And there's Berric!"

The pale wizard paused on the

top step, alerted by Petra's voice. He stared down with a triumphant smile.

"So, you destroyed the maze – and now you think to destroy me?" he cried. "I think not! Falkor! Deal with these irritants!"

The snake's head appeared at the high entrance. His glittering eyes fixed on Tom and his two companions. He let out a sharp hiss and slid off the stairs, his lithe body twining around a column, scales glinting blood-red as he slithered down.

"I'll deal with Berric!" Tom shouted, running for the stairway. "Distract Falkor – but don't try to fight him!"

Falkor glided down the column, jaws gaping and poisonous fangs dripping. Tom raced for the stairs, bounding up them four at a time, only a hair's breadth ahead of Falkor's clashing jaws.

Tom heard a crackling sound. He turned and saw a blue light shimmering around Falkor's head. Petra stood at the foot of the stairs, her hand stretched out, blue fire leaping from her fingertips.

The witch's powers had returned.

The Beast spun around, hissing angrily. Petra and Elenna raced away as Falkor pursued them across the floor.

Falkor is under Berric's control – I have to get up there and defeat him before the Beast kills my friends!

Tom pounded up the stairs as they wound around the fortress. Every now and then he caught a glimpse through a window of Elenna and Petra playing a deadly game of cat and mouse with the Beast. Elenna was firing arrows that glanced off the Beast's scales, and Petra was flinging blue fire that only served to make Falkor all the more angry.

Tom continued climbing the long stairway. Even with the power of the leg armour, he was finding it harder and harder to lift his feet as the stair wound up to dizzying heights.

At last he came to the entrance that led back into the fortress. Gasping for breath, his whole body burning with exhaustion, he stumbled in, sword and shield ready.

The statue of Rufus confronted him

on the lofty platform. Tom's heart skipped a beat. The hands had been broken off and the great scythe was gone!

"Are you looking for this?" Berric stepped from behind the statue, the weapon in his hands. "Would you like to see how it works?"

Berric fired a stream of red fire from the blade. Tom was only just able to get his shield up in time, the flames forcing him backwards.

Laughing, Berric stepped forwards, a river of fire scorching the air between them. Tom gasped as the fire formed itself into burning fingers that wrenched the shield from his arm. He dropped to one knee, seeing his shield spinning down through the air.

"Now do you understand your true peril?" Berric snarled. "You may have defeated powerful wizards in the past – but now I have the scythe in my hands, I am invincible!"

But Tom would never give up. He sprang forwards, closing in on Berric.

"I've been threatened with death many times," Tom shouted. "But I'm still here – and my enemies are all gone!"

He brought his sword down in a sweeping arc, but Berric easily deflected Tom's attack with the scythe.

Berric stepped back and twisted the scythe's blade so that Tom's sword was almost wrenched from his grip. "Surrender now and I'll give you a quick death." Berric's voice was calm as he backed smoothly away, stepping off the platform and floating in mid-air. "Come – follow me if you can."

Tom stared at him, astonished and alarmed by this display of Berric's new powers. What other, deadlier

magic did the scythe hold?

Berric laughed. "Can you fly, Tom?" Then he twisted the scythe and blasted flames at Tom's feet.

Tom staggered and fell, red fire leaping all around him as he plunged helplessly downwards.

4

CAUGHT IN THE COILS

Berric's laughter echoed in Tom's ears as he fell. As the floor rushed up towards him, his heart was torn by despair. He had failed to protect Avantia from this new terrible danger, and that was a pain deeper than any he had ever suffered before.

The air shrieking in his ears, he glimpsed Elenna, staring wide-eyed, her hands to her mouth.

But a moment before he smashed to the floor, he came to a shuddering halt. He gasped, turning his head to see Petra, a green light extending from her hand to Tom. The witch had saved him!

He would live to fight on!

Petra twirled her fingers and Tom settled to the floor. "You owe me now," she said, as Tom got up. Then her voice rose to a shriek. "Behind you!"

Her cry was almost drowned out by a sudden ear-splitting hissing at his back. Tom spun around and found himself staring into the red eyes of the snake-Beast. He lifted his sword, but Falkor's head lunged down, poison spraying from jutting fangs.

Tom leaped aside, but the snout struck him in the chest, tossing him backwards across the chamber. He skidded along the floor, pain searing through his midriff.

Ignoring the agony, Tom scrambled to his feet, racing towards Falkor, his sword raised above his head.

Elenna joined in the attack. Running towards Falkor, she fitted an arrow to her bow, but before she could loose it, a blast of blood-red fire exploded at her feet, throwing her backwards.

"Elenna!" Anger flared in Tom's heart as he heard cold laughter from above. Berric hung in the air above him, brewing more flames in the hollow of his hand.

Tom jumped high, slashing the air with his sword. But the wizard floated just out of reach of Tom's blade.

Tom saw his shield lying close by. Praying that Elenna wasn't badly hurt, he snatched up his shield and sprang to his feet.

"I'm ready for you now!" he shouted.

"Face me if you dare!"

Berric aimed the scythe at Tom. "I dare," he cried. "And you die!"

But before Berric could hurl a spell, Petra tossed a crackling ball of purple fire up at him. The wizard jerked back as the fiery ball scorched past his chest and exploded against the wall of the fortress. Chunks of masonry tumbled down, crashing and splintering on the floor.

Petra flung a second flaming ball, but Berric was ready for her now. With a contemptuous sneer, he used the scythe to bat it back to her.

Petra threw her arms up as the ball erupted before her face.

"Is that the best you can do?" shouted Berric.

Panic twisted Petra's face as the
ball expanded around her. She flung
spears of blue light from her fingers,
but her spells shattered uselessly on
the inner shell of the shimmering
globe. She was trapped.

Tom ran to her, striking the sphere
with his sword – but the blade

glanced uselessly off.

"You cannot escape," Berric cried. "Now witness the power of the scythe!" He pointed the curved blade at the witch. The globe distorted as the scythe's power struck it.

Petra writhed, screaming as the purple lightning was drawn up into the scythe's blade.

Tom spun around, intending to leap up at Berric, but the massive body of Falkor slid between them, blocking his way.

The ball of power faded around Petra and she dropped to her knees, staring at her empty hands. "He's taken my magic!" he cried.

The legend was true!

"Tell me, Tom," sneered Berric.

"How can you fight someone who becomes more powerful every moment?"

Tom brandished his sword above Falkor's slithering back. He had never felt such hatred for anyone before. "While there's blood in my veins, I will never give up!" he shouted.

"Then the blood needs to come out of your veins!" howled Berric. "Falkor – tear this boy to shreds!"

Falkor's head darted forwards, but this time Tom was ready for the attack. He jumped high, somersaulting over the snout and twisting in mid-air so that he came down feet-first on the snake's head. He sprinted along Falkor's spine, keeping ahead of the slavering fangs as the Beast twisted and writhed to get at him.

Tom hardly had time to think. He had to keep ahead of those poisonous fangs and pray that Berric would hold back to watch the Beast kill him.

A hazardous plan formed in Tom's mind. Perhaps he could get the Beast to entangle himself among the pillars.

He flung himself from Falkor's tail, racing past his head and diving behind a pillar. He sprinted across open ground to another pillar, Falkor following close. Tom ducked behind the pillar at the last moment and the Beast's head pounded into the stone, shaking the whole fortress.

Tom glanced across the chamber and saw Elenna struggling to get up.

He dived behind a third column, venom splashing all around him, sizzling as it ate into the stone.

"Run while you can!" Berric's mocking voice rang out above Falkor's hissing. "Let's see how well you fight when the Beast's fangs pierce your heart!"

Tom ignored the taunts. For his dangerous plan to succeed, he had to weave in and out of the columns, forcing Falkor to follow. He glanced back. *Yes, it's working!* The Beast's long lithe body was winding through the columns.

Tom paused, turning and bracing himself for Falkor's strike. He knew he had to time this to perfection. His taut muscles uncoiled and he

sprang up, landing with one foot on
the top of the Beast's head, bounding
forwards, down the back and away.

Falkor twisted back, coiling tightly
around the column. Tom raced
around the nearest column, the fangs
snapping at his back. He hurled

himself sideways, his sword ringing against Falkor's fangs. Pools of venom burned the floor beneath his feet. He made one last desperate lunge forward, the fangs rasping across his shoulders.

The Beast's head jerked to a sudden halt. Tom spun around. Falkor was thrashing, his head stretched upwards as he fought to get free.

Tom jumped back as one of the pillars cracked and broke apart. A low rumbling sounded from high above as the pillar tottered and fell. Another column crumbled as Falkor's body thrashed.

The Beast is more powerful than I expected! Falkor is going to bring the whole fortress down!

Blocks of stone thundered around Tom, smashing on the floor in billowing clouds of dust.

Berric stared upwards, the smirk gone from his face as he saw cracks opening in the roof of the fortress.

"Falkor, stop!" he howled.

But the enraged Beast only writhed and fought harder to get loose, dragging down column after column in his furious battle to reach Tom.

Cra-a-a-ack!

Tom glanced up. An entire section of the roof had broken away, bringing the statue of Rufus down with it. A mass of stone was tumbling down towards him.

Falkor is too powerful – I've killed us all!

5

TERROR OF THE WHITE FIRE

Tom dived sideways, tucking and rolling as he heard the crash of stone smashing on the ground. Shrouds of dust billowed up and jagged stone fragments ricocheted off the trembling walls. He could see Falkor, still struggling among the ruins, the Beast's head straining upwards as the columns tumbled.

Then he saw something that gave him new hope.

Berric had been knocked to the ground. The young wizard picked himself up, shaking his head – not badly hurt, but dazed and off-guard.

Tom bounded forwards, hammering his shoulder into Berric's stomach, sending the scythe flying from the wizard's hand.

Berric lay on his back, grimacing in pain. Tom stood over him, the point of his sword at the wizard's throat.

"Yield or face the consequences."

A sly grin spread across Berric's face. Tom saw his fingers moving. *The wizard still has magic in him!*

Just then, his sword began to burn his fingers. With a cry, he dropped

it. Berric kicked Tom in the chest,
sending him staggering backwards.

Berric sprang up, his arms raised,
fingers spreading. Pieces of stone rose
from the floor and spun towards Tom
as though hurled from a slingshot.
He raised his shield, blocking the

pummelling shards, but there were too many of them. One burst through his defences and struck him a numbing blow on the shoulder.

"Where is the scythe?" Berric howled.

From the corner of his eye, Tom saw Elenna rising painfully from the floor. There was no sign of the witch.

There was a crack and a deep rumble as Falkor finally tore free of the remaining columns. The Beast glided menacingly through the swirling dust cloud, but then paused, turning his head from side to side. His eyes shifted uneasily from Berric to Tom.

Tom flashed a glance at his sword as a sibilant voice echoed in his head.

Who has awoken me?

It was Falkor's voice, entering Tom's

mind through the power of the red jewel. The ancient Beast was confused and hesitant.

"Falkor! Attack!" howled Berric, pointing at Tom.

The huge eyes blinked, the mouth opening and closing as the long tongue flickered. But Falkor didn't obey Berric's command. Instead, the Beast turned and slithered across the floor to the broken statue of Rufus.

The Beast stared at the statue's head, deep sadness filling his eyes.

He recognises his old master. Hope ignited in Tom's heart. *Berric has no more power over the Beast!*

Surely now Falkor would help him defeat the wizard.

A beam of harsh white light shot

across the chamber, striking Falkor and driving the Beast writhing back, hissing in pain. As Tom watched in horror, the great snake coiled up, his jaws gaping and eyes brimming with agony as the white fire played along his shuddering body.

Tom spun around, following the ribbon of white fire back to its source.

Petra was poised atop a heap of rubble, the Scythe of Power in her hands. She directed the fire at Falkor from the curved blade, eyes gleaming and an ugly grin twisting her face.

"Petra, stop!" Tom shouted, running towards her. "Berric's spell is broken!"

Petra let out a howl of laughter as the flames gnawed at the Beast's pain-wracked body.

"I don't care about that white-haired fool!" Petra shouted. "The power of the scythe is mine! Watch, Tom, as I slay the Beast!"

Berric was on his knees, staring up at her in disbelief. He flung his arms

forwards, magically hurling chunks of stone at her. Petra tossed her hair and the stones crumbled to dust.

"Pathetic!" she shouted. "Don't try my patience, Berric – or I'll turn the fire on you!" Her eyes flashed with madness. "I've waited a long time for this! Those doddering fools in the Circle of Wizards will be no match for me!" Her voice rose to a shriek. "I'll rule every kingdom!"

"Listen to yourself!" shouted Tom. "The scythe has driven you mad!"

"Idiot!" spat the witch. "Don't you understand yet? I only came on your Quest to get the scythe." Her laughter rang through the fortress. "I knew you and your feeble-minded companion would fight like furies to get through the maze. I just waited for the perfect moment to strike!"

"I was wrong about you,"Tom cried. "You're not mad – you're pure evil!"

"Flattery will get you nowhere!" Petra laughed, releasing one hand from the scythe and aiming her outstretched fingers at Tom. "And now that you've served your purpose, it's time for you to—"

A figure leaped up behind the witch and brought a rock down on the back of her head. Petra dropped in mid-sentence, the scythe falling from her hand, the river of fire fading away.

Elenna stood over the unconscious witch, the rock still in her fist.

"I don't like to say 'I told you so' about her," said Elenna. "But I did."

6

SCYTHE AND SCALES

A ferocious hissing reverberated
through the crumbling fortress. Tom
turned to see Falkor, mad with pain
and rage, lashing wildly around.
Its tail struck Berric, spinning
him across the floor. Falkor's head
smashed into the last standing pillars,
sending them crashing down.

Tom rushed forwards, touching his

fingers to the red jewel. *Stop, Falkor –*
no one will hurt you now.

But Tom could see from the burning
rage in Falkor's eyes that the agonies
of the white fire had driven him out
of his mind. Words couldn't stop him
– only action would.

Tom vaulted on to the Beast's back,
clawing his way up the scales and
running towards the head. It was
hard to keep his footing as Falkor
squirmed and coiled, trying to bite
him with fangs that dripped venom.

One scratch and not even all the
magic in the kingdom could save me.

He stood behind the Beast's head,
feet spread wide, and brought his
shield down hard, hoping to snap
Falkor out of his fury. But the blow

only made the Beast angrier. He jerked his head up, tossing Tom so he fell among the rubble.

Tom shook off the pain, gripping his sword and shield, bracing himself for an attack. But Falkor turned away and slithered towards Elenna.

She tried to run, but the snake's tail looped around her waist and dragged her down off the pile of debris.

Before Tom could run to her defence, another section of the roof fell in, a huge chunk of masonry smashing down on top of him and pinning his legs. He choked on thick dustas he struggled to drag himself free. It was hopeless – broken edges of stone dug into him, and pain knifed through him at every movement.

As the dust cleared, he saw Berric stumble to his feet and stagger towards the exit. He glanced towards Elenna, her face twisted with desperation as she tried to wrench herself free of the tightening coils.

"Berric! Help her!" he called.

The wizard ignored his plea.

He'll let her die – I'm the only one who can save her.

Tom strained against the stone that pinned him, sweat dripping from his face. His muscles burned, every sinew seared by pain.

The stone shifted a little. Gasping, Tom wrenched his legs free.

He scrambled to his feet, grabbing his sword as he ran at the Beast. He jumped on to Falkor's tail, digging

the point in between the scales, trying
to find soft flesh under the armour.
If he could only hurt Falkor enough
to make him loosen his grip, Elenna
might be able to wrench herself free.

His friend's cries were growing

weaker – the Beast was squeezing the life out of her!

Tom focused on the red jewel.

We're not your enemies, Falkor – we're here to help you!

Elenna's face was turning purple, the veins on her neck standing out. Her lips moved, but Tom couldn't hear what she was saying.

Her eyes rolled. With her last breath, she was trying to tell him something. Tom followed the line of her eyes to the scythe which lay on the floor, just out of reach.

Of course!

Tom flung himself at the scythe and snatched it up, swinging the blade at Falkor. The tip of the blade rang on the Beast's forehead and glanced off, the handle slipping from Tom's hands.

The scythe fell to the floor – even Rufus's weapon wasn't sharp enough to pierce those armoured scales.

Falkor reared up, tongue flickering as he towered over Tom. But then he hesitated, head swaying. Tom saw that the place the scythe had touched was turning grey. He watched in astonishment as the grey stain spread over Falkor's head. The Beast's body jerked, shuddering from head to tail. The coils loosened around Elenna and she fell to the floor.

The venom stopped dripping from the fangs, poisonous liquid hardening in the gaping mouth. The furious red light faded from the Beast's eyes.

The grey hue spread along Falkor's

body. Tom could see the coils stiffening, the colour fading from the scales as they fused together. The Beast's head dropped, lifeless eyes closing as he turned back to stone.

Tom heard a voice in his head.

Peace again!

Tom bowed his head, glad that the ancient Beast was sleeping once more.

A rumbling from above warned Tom that they were not yet safe. Stones tumbled down. The fortress was close to complete collapse.

He ran, stooping to grab Petra and dragging her along with him. Elenna ran to his side, her clothes torn and filthy and her face pale.

The lintel of the door had a long crack in it. The walls above

shuddered and shook, debris
tumbling down all around them.

Tom glanced back at the scythe –
even buried under heaps of stone, it
was still a source of terrible danger.

I must make sure no one else ever wields its power!

He turned to Elenna. "Take Petra to safety," he said, shoving the witch into Elenna's arms. "I have one more thing to do inside the fortress!"

"No! You'll be killed!" cried Elenna.

Tom dashed back in, past the falling rock. He grasped the scythe and brought it down on his knee. It broke in two with a spurt of silver fire.

"This will never again fall into evil hands!" he shouted, flinging the broken pieces down. He turned and dived out through the gateway as more masonry crashed at his heels.

As Tom got to his feet, his heart sank. Elenna stood, body stiff, caught in a ring of magic flame coming from

Berric's outstretched hand. Petra lay crumpled on the ground at his feet.

"Give me the scythe, or she dies in agony!" shouted the wizard.

"I can't – it's in there!" said Tom, pointing back through the entrance.

Rage and panic filled Berric's face. He dropped his arm and the blue fire faded away. Berric plunged back towards the smoke-filled doorway and Elenna staggered, gasping for breath as she was released.

"Don't go in there!" shouted Tom, snatching at the wizard's flying robes.

"The scythe's power must be mine!" Berric vanished into the fortress.

A moment later, Tom heard his cry as the ceiling caved in and smoke poured from the ruined gatehouse.

7

BERRIC'S SCYTHE

Tom turned from the smoking remains of the ancient fortress.

Berric was blinded by his lust for power.

He and Elenna carried Petra between them as they picked a path through the slush where ice maze had stood. Behind them, the fortress ruins lay under a plume of dark smoke.

They made for the witch's portal,

hanging in the air beyond the maze.

They were halfway there when Petra's eyelids fluttered open. "What happened?" she mumbled. "Oww! My head hurts!"

"That would be my fault," said Elenna. "You said you wanted to rule the world with the power of Rufus's scythe. So I hit you with a rock."

Petra pulled free, glaring at Elenna. Then her expression softened. "I was only play-acting to fool Berric," she said. "I never meant any real harm."

"We'll let the judge decide that," said Tom. "You're going to stand trial."

"There's no need for that," Petra said, her face draining of colour. "Let's talk this through."

"We've heard enough lies," snapped

Elenna, grabbing Petra and dragging her along. The portal was only a little way off now, shimmering in the air.

"What happened to Berric?" Petra asked, struggling as Tom took hold of her other arm.

"He ran back into the fortress," Tom said. "He must have been crushed."

Petra glanced back, her eyes widening. "Think again."

As Tom and Elenna watched, a figure came staggering through the grey clouds surrounding the fortress. His clothes were filthy and torn, his hair was matted and blood ran from a cut on his forehead.

"He survived!" breathed Tom. He had never wished for the wizard's death – but he could not let the wizard go free, not after all the evil he had done. Tom drew his sword – the fight was not over yet.

Berric raised the broken scythe above his head. "I will have my revenge on you!" he shrieked.

"I think not!" Elenna released Petra, nocking an arrow to her bow.

"You can't kill him," Tom said. "The scythe is useless now."

Elenna gave a quick smile as she loosed the arrow. It flew straight and true, missing Berric and striking the top of the lever that she had pulled to turn the maze to water.

The lever clanged down and snapped off at the base. Berric twisted around, staring at it.

"What have you done?" he roared.

Even as he spoke, a blast of icy air came howling across the ground, sending Tom, Elenna and the witch stumbling back, and almost knocking Berric off his feet.

Narrowing his eyes against the deadly cold, Tom saw the waters of the maze rising up all around the fortress in slender fountains.

"Nice shooting!" exclaimed Petra.

Through the torrents of water, Tom could just make out Berric running back and forth, brandishing the broken scythe. The fountains froze in mid-air and the wizard was lost from view. There was a crackling sound as the water became solid walls of ice.

By some ancient magic, the maze had re-formed itself. The lever was broken and Berric was trapped inside.

"That should keep him busy for a while," Elenna said with a grin.

"It's time for us to go back," said Tom, turning to the portal. "Petra – you're coming with us."

"Guess again!" The witch giggled as she jumped away, her fingers twirling.

A diamond-shaped portal opened up behind her. "See you soon," she said as she stepped through.

"No!" Tom lunged for her, but his fingers snatched thin air as Petra's mocking laughter faded and the portal vanished. "She got away!"

"Something tells me we haven't seen the last of Petra," said Elenna. "Come on, we need to head home. Someone has to explain to the circle that Daltec wasn't to blame for the destruction on the plains."

They turned to the original portal. Tom could faintly hear Berric shouting from behind the walls of the ice maze, but he couldn't make out what the trapped wizard was saying.

Dire and deadly threats, I suppose.

But without Falkor, he will never find his way out of the maze.

With that thought, Tom led Elenna through the portal.

A small celebration was taking place in the throne room of King Hugo's Palace. Two days had passed since Tom and Elenna had returned to explain the truth to the Circle of Wizards. Sorella, the new judge, had officially pardoned Daltec and welcomed him to his rightful seat.

They were gathered at a long table, laden with food and drink. Daltec stood at the end of the table, smiling as he made plates of food appear from nowhere in front of the guests.

Laughter and applause filled the air.

"It's nice to see him having a good time," Elenna murmured, and Tom nodded in agreement.

"How does it feel to be proved innocent?" he asked the wizard.

"It is the best feeling in the world," Daltec replied. "And it's all thanks to you and Elenna!" For a moment, as he smiled at them, his hand faltered. A goblet that was floating in front of Queen Aroha trembled and wine slopped, almost splashing her.

"Oops! So sorry, Your Majesty," gasped Daltec. "Juggling so many things is tricky."

Queen Aroha smiled and soon everyone was laughing with her. Daltec gave a red-faced grin, bringing

his hands down slowly so that every plate and cup came to rest safely.

As they ate, Aduro leaned towards Tom. "The Circle of Wizards made magical searches of all the known kingdoms," he said. "There has been no sighting of Petra anywhere."

"Good," said Elenna. "Let's hope she

stays lost for a long time."

"Your Majesties," Daltec was standing again. "Fellow witches and wizards, please join me in a toast!" He looked gratefully at Tom and Elenna. "To our two heroes – without their help, I would never have been accepted into the Circle of Wizards!"

"You have Rufus and his scythe to thank for that," Tom said as the others drank. "Who would have thought our victory over Berric would be made possible by a long-dead sorcerer?"

And he drank along with all the others, glad that Falkor was sleeping again. The Kingdom of Avantia was safe from evil. For now, at least…

THE END

CONGRATULATIONS, YOU HAVE COMPLETED THIS QUEST!

At the end of each chapter you were awarded a special gold coin.
The QUEST in this book was worth an amazing 14 coins.

Look at the Beast Quest totem picture inside the back cover of this book to see how far you've come in your journey to become

MASTER OF THE BEASTS.

The more books you read, the more coins you will collect!

Do you want your own
Beast Quest Totem?
1. Cut out and collect the coin below
2. Go to the Beast Quest website
3. Download and print out your totem
4. Add your coin to the totem
www.beastquest.co.uk/totem

Have you read the latest series of Beast Quest? Read on for a sneak peek at KRYTOR THE BLOOD BAT!

CHAPTER ONE

HOME!

"Ouch!" Elenna yelped, hopping on to one foot. "I've got a stone in my boot!"

Tom grinned as he watched his friend retrieve the stone and hurl it away.

"Just a little pebble," he said, pleased to have a moment to rest. "I can't believe you're complaining so much. We've been through worse."

"A lot worse." Elenna laughed. "Why couldn't Daltec magic us back from Gwildor?"

She has a point, Tom thought. The journey back to Avantia had been long and gruelling, taking them over both land and sea.

Tom lifted his chin. Being a Master of Beasts meant doing difficult things. This journey home was just part of that. He pointed up ahead at the soaring towers of King Hugo's palace in the City. "Look, not that far now."

Read KRYTOR THE BLOOD BAT
to find out more!

FIGHT THE BEASTS,
FEAR THE MAGIC

Are you a BEAST QUEST mega fan?
Do you want to know about all the latest news,
competitions and books before anyone else?

Then join our Quest Club!

Visit the BEAST QUEST website
and sign up today!

www.beastquest.co.uk

CALLING ALL BEAST QUEST FANS - DRAW YOUR FAVOURITE BEAST!

Beast Quest is turning 10 next year and we want YOU to help us celebrate this special birthday. We're looking for drawings of your favourite Beasts to make into a special Beast Quest logo.

For each drawing we receive we will enter the artist into a special prize draw, where five lucky winners can win Beast Quest goodies!

To enter send your entries to:
Beast Quest Drawing Competition
Hachette Children's Books
Carmelite House
50 Victoria Embankment
London
EC47 0DZ

Closing date for entries 31st December 2016
For full terms and conditions please go to
www.hachettechildrensdigital.co.uk/terms/